John Lydgate, Francis J. Child

The Child of Bristowe

a legend of the fourteenth century

John Lydgate, Francis J. Child

The Child of Bristowe
a legend of the fourteenth century

ISBN/EAN: 9783337392260

Printed in Europe, USA, Canada, Australia, Japan

Cover: Foto ©Andreas Hilbeck / pixelio.de

More available books at **www.hansebooks.com**

THE CHILD OF BRISTOWE

A Legend

OF THE

FOURTEENTH CENTURY

CAMBRIDGE

JOHN WILSON AND SON

University Press

1886

Affectionately offered to

EPES SARGENT DIXWELL

and

MARY INGERSOLL BOWDITCH DIXWELL.

THIS sweet old tale has been modernized enough to make it easy reading, without sacrifice, I hope, of its pristine flavor.

F. J. CHILD.

THE CHILD OF BRISTOWE.

———◦◦⚬◦◦———

I FOUND it written in oldë hand
That sometime dwelled in Engëland
   A squire mickle of might;
He had castles, towns, and towers,
Forests fair, and fields with flowers,
   Wild beasts for his delight.
Law he followed a great while;
Poor men he learnëd to beguile,
   All against the right;
Mickle goods he gathered had,
All with treason and deedës bad:
   He feared not God Almight.

The goods that he had gathered then
Were got from many poorë men,
  The mostë part with wrong;
He had a sone, sholde be his heir;
Of shape he seemly was and fair,
  Of limbës large and strong.
So much his mind was on that child,
He recktë not whom he beguiled,
  Worldly good to get,
And all to make his sone so rich
That no other might be his match: `
  On this his thought was set.

When the child was twelve year old
His father sent him to be schooled,
  To learn to be a clerk;
So long to clergy he applies,
Till he becomes both learned and wise,
  And dreads all deedës dark.
The father said to his sonë dear,
" Law thou now shalt learn a year,
  And it cost me twenty mark;
For ever the better shalt thou be;
Then shall no man beguilen thee
  Neither in word nor work."

The child answered when this he saw,
" They fare full well that learn no law,
  And so 1 hope to do;
That life will I never lead,
To put my soul in so great drede,
  To makë God my foe.
To slay my soulë, it were ruth;
Any science that is truth,
  I shall assent thereto;
But to forego my soulë's health
For any winning of worldly wealth,
  That will I never mo.

" It hath ever been my choice
To lead my life in merchandise,
  To learn to buy and sell;
The money got in way of trade,
It seems to me, is truly made:
  Therewith wolde I deal.
Here at Bristowe dwelleth one
Who is holden a just, true man,
  As I have heard tell;
His prentis seven year will I be,
For to learn his mystery,
  And with him will I dwell."

The squire unto Bristowe rade,
And with the merchant covenant made
    Seven year to keep his sone;
Gold he gave him, great plenty,
The child sholde his apprentis be,
    His science for to con.
The child took full well to lore;
In God his love was evermore,
    As he had begun;
He grew up courteous of tongue,
All merchants loved him, old and young,
    In that country, every one.

Leave we the prentis at Bristowe,
And of his father speak we now,
    That was so stiff and bold;
So high advanced now was he,
There was no man in that country
    Durst do but as he wolde.
Ever he practised usury,
Nor lent but on security
    Of increase double-fold;
Tithes he never liste to pay,
And if the parsons ought wolde say,
    He gave them comfort cold.

All things come to an end at last;
God on him such sickness cast,
   He might no longer abide;
On his death-bed then he lay,
And drew toward his dying day,
   For all his power and pride.
Then he sent for knights and squires,
Which were his neighbors and compeers
   In that country-side;
He said among them every one,
"Sirs, my life is almost gone,
   It may not be denied."

There was no man in that country
That his executor wolde be,
   For good nor ill: for why?
They said his goods were gotten so,
They wolde not have therewith to do,
   For dread of God on high.
He prayed them; but they answered nay.
"Alas," said he, "and welaway!"
   With a rueful cry;
After his only sone he sent,
Unto Bristowe, verament,
   But seven miles thence, hard by.

The child to the chamber took his way
Where his father on his death-bed lay,
     And asked him of his cheer;
"Sone," he said, "welcome to me;
I lie here, as thou mayst see;
     My last day nigheth near.
But, sone, thou must be mine heir,
Of all my landës good and fair,
     Of lordships, gold, and gear;
Therefore, sone, now pray I thee
Mine attorney that thou be,
     When I am brought to bier."

The sone answered with wordës mild,
"Father, ye see I am but a child;
     Discretion have I not
To take such a charge on me;
By my faith, that shall not be:
     I have not wit for that.
Here be knightës and esquires,
Which were your neighbors and compeers,
     And many a worthy wight;
To take on me, if I sholde choose,
What all these worthy men refuse,
     I were a fool outright."

"Sone," he said, "thou scapest not so,
That thou shalt learn before thou go;"
   He said, "I chargë thee,
As before God thou wilt answére,
And as thou wilt my blessing bear,
   My attorney that thou be."
"Ah, father! ye bind me with a charge,
And I shall bind you with one as large
   As ye now bind me:
The same day fortnight that ye pass,
Appear, I charge you, in this place,
   Your spirit let me see.

"For ye have bounden me so sare,
Your command, how so I fare,
   Do I needës must;
Therefore I charge you to appear,
That I may see your soulë here,
   Whether it be saved or lost:
And that thou do no harm to me,
Nor no one that shall come with thee."
   "Sone," he said, "I assent;
But alas that I was born,
That mannës soulë sholde be lorn
   For any gold or rent!"

The parish priest anon was sought:
The sacrament with him he brought,
  That died for mannës wo;
The father shrived him with hertë sore,
And cried God mercy evermore,
  As it was time to do.
When God's time was, he went his way;
His sonës song was welaway!
  For him his heart did wring;
He sought about from town to town
For priests and men of religïoun, .
  The dirges for to sing.

When they had brought him to his grave,
His sone, that thought his soul to save,
  If God wolde give him leave,
All the substance his father had,
He sold it off, and money made,
  And labored morn and eve.
He inquired in that country then
Where almës might be done to men,
  And largely wolde he give;
Roads and bridges wolde he make,
And poor men, for Goddës sake,
  He gave them great relief.

Who askëd aught, content was made;
Thirty trentals of masses said
   For his father's sake;
He stopt not till he had spent
All his father's treasure and rent,
   Amends to God to make.
By the time the fortnight's end was come
His gold was gone, all and some.
   Many men of him spake;
And all the movables that there were,
He gave away, and wolde not spare,
   To poor men that wolde take.

When that fortnight had come to end,
The child gan to the chamber wend
   Where his father died;
Many good prayers did he say,
Adown he kneelëd half a day,
   His father to abide.
Between midday and none there came
A blast of thunder and lightning flame
   Through the wallës wide,
As all the place on fire sholde be:
The child said, " Benedicite ! "
   And fast on God he cried.

And as he was in his prayëre,
Anon before him did appear,
    Foul sights and sounds between,
His father, burning as a coal,
Whom a devil by the neck did haul
    In a burning chain.
The child said: "I conjure thee,
Whateer thou be, to speak to me."
    The other said again:
"I am thy father, that thee begat;
Thou mayst behold now mine estate,
    Lo now I dwell in pain!"

The child said: "Ah, woe is me,
In this plight that I you see!
    Mine heart it woundeth sore;"
"Sone, thus am I now bested
For the falseness," so he said,
    "That I used evermore.
My goods were gotten wrongfully;
And unless restored they be,
    With amends therefor,
An hundred years it shall be so;
Give me my troth, and let me go;
    Till then my soul is lore."

"Nay, father, thus it shall not be;
In better estate I will you see,
  If God will give me grace;
But ye your troth to me shall plight
This same day a fortënight
  To apperen in this place,
And I shall labor, if I may,
To bring your soul in better way,
  If I have life and space."
He promised him, all in great haste;
With that there came a thunder-blast,
  And both their way did pass.

The child had never so great sorrow;
He rose up upon the morrow,
  To Bristowe gan he wend;
To his master he gan say,
"I have served you many a day,
  For God's love be my friend.
My father out of this world is past;
I am come to you in haste,
  I have ever found you kind;
I need a little sum of gold;
My heritage it shall be sold,
  Top and root and rind."

His master said: "What need for thee
To sell thine estate so hastily?
    It were not for thy behoof;
If any bargain thou have bought,
For gold and silver care thou nought,
    I shall lend thee right enough.
Have a hundred mark, if that thou lack.
Seven years — I will not ask it back —
    Wherefore advise thee now;
For if thou sell thine heritage,
That sholde help thee, in thy young age,
    An unwise man art thou."

"Gramercy," he said, " my master kind,
This was the proffer of a friend,
    But truly it shall be sold;
A better bargain ye shall have
Than any man, so God me save,
    For needs I must have gold."
He said, "What is it worth a year?"
"An hundred mark of money clear,
    The steward this me told; "
"Then shall I give thee three hundred pound,
Every penny whole and sound: "
    The young man said, " I hold."

" Derë master, I you pray,
Take the deeds, fetch me my pay,
　For I must home again;
I have affairs in an other place.
I pray you for a fortnight's space;
　I shall repay, certain."
His maister loved the child so well,
The gold he fetcht, and did him tell.
　Then was the child right fain;
He took the money, and went his way:
Heavy on his heart his father lay,
　That was in so much pain.

In church and market, all about,
Where his father lived, the child sent out
　His proclamation:
What man or woman did there belong,
To whom his father had done wrong,
　They sholde come to the sone,
And he wolde make amends therefor,
And their goods again restore,
　To every man his own.
Even as they came he wolde repay,
And bade them for his father pray,
　To bliss that he might gon.

When the fortnight's end was come,
His gold was gone, all and some,
  And he had no more;
Into the chamber he went that tide,
The same in which his father died,
  And kneelëd on the floor.
And as he was praying there,
The spirit gan to him appear,
  Right as he did before,
Save there was no chain red hot:
Black he was, but he burnt not,
  Though in anguish sore.

"Welcome, father," said the child;
And besought him with wordës mild,
  "Tell me of your estate."
"Sone," he said, "the better for thee.
Blessed may the timë be
  That ever I thee begat!
Thou hast relieved me of much wo:
Fallen away the chain is now,
  And the fiery heat;
But yet still I dwell in pain,
And ever so I must remain,
  Till I fulfil my date."

"Father," he said, "I charge you tell
What is most against you still,
  And gives you most distress."
"Tithes and offerings, sone," he said,
"For them I never truly paid;
  Wherefore pain may not cease.
Unless it be restored again,
To every church its due, certain,
  And also with increase,
For me all that thou dost pray
Helps me not to the uttermost day
  The value of two peas.

"Therefore I pray thee, hastily,
Give me the troth I left with thee,
  And let me wend my way."
"Nay, father," he said, "ye get it nought;
Other help there shall be sought:
  Yet again will I essay.
But your troth ye shall me plight
This same time a fortënight
  To come to keep your day;
Ye shall appear here in this place,
And I shall try, with Goddës grace,
  To better you, if I may."

The spirit wentë forth in sorrow;
The child rose upon the morrow,
  He tarried for no let.
He went to Bristowe for to find,
As before, his master kind;
  And said, when him he met:
"When I have need, I come to you.
Master, but ye help me now,
  Sorrow my heart will eat;
A litel sum of gold I lack,
Another bargain I wolde make:"
  With that began to greet.

His master said: "Thou art a fool!
Thou hast been at some bad school;
  By my faith, I hold thee mad!
For thou hast been playing at the dice,
Or else by some other vice
  Hast lost what thou hast had.
Thou hast nought that thou mayst sell;
All is gone, as I hear tell:
  Thy management is bad."
He said unto his master free,
"*My body* I will sell to thee,
  For ever to be thy lad.

"Bondsman to thee I will me bind,
Me and mine to the worldës end,
  To help me in this need."
He said, "How much then woldst thou have?"
"Forty marks, and ye wolde vouchsafe, —
  That sholde suffice indeed;
I hope that shall my cares dispell."
The burgess loved the child right well,
  Let him no longer plead;
Forty pound he gan him bring:
"Sone, here is more than thy asking,
  Almighty God thee speed!"

"Gramercy, sir," the child did say,
"God requite you, who best may;
  True ye shall me find;
I have a thing or two to do;
A fortnight give me leave to go:
  Still have I found you kind."
He gave him leave, he went his way;
Thinking on his father aye,
  He was not out of his mind;
To all the churches in that country
Where his father had dwelt the child went he,
  He left not one behind.

He made atonement to every one;
By that time his money was gone,
   They could ask of him no more;
But as he went along the street,
With a poor man he did meet,
   Almost naked and frore.
Down on knees the poor man goes:
" For a quarter of corn your father owes,
   Which I feared to ask him for,
For your father's soulës sake,
Some amends I pray you make,
   For him that Mary bore ! "

"Welaway ! " said the youngë man,
" For my gold and silver is gone;
   I have not wherewith to pay; "
Off his clothës he gan take,
And put them on the poor man's back;
   For his father bade him pray.
Hose and shoon he gave him too;
In shirt and breech himself did go,
   He had no clothës gay;
Into the chamber that same tide
He wentë, where his father died,
   And kneelëd half a day.

When he had kneeled and prayed long,
He thought he heard the joyfullest song
  That earthly man might hear;
After the song he saw a light,
As 't were a thousand torches bright,
  It shone so fair and clear.
In that radiance there did stand
A naked child, in angel's hand,
  And these words said he:
" Sone," he saidë, " be thou blest,
That ever thou begotten wast,
  And all that shall come from thee."

" Father," the sone said, " well is me
In such plight that I you see;
  I hope God shall you save!"
" Sone," he said, " I go to bliss;
God Almighty requite thee this,
  And grant thee thy goods to have.
Thou hast stript thyself full bare,
Me to free from sorrow and care;
  My troth, good sone, I crave;"
" Freely have thy troth," said he;
" And for thy blessing I pray thee,
  If so thou wilt vouchsafe."

"All such blessing mayst thou have
As her sone Our Lady gave;
  And mine on thee I lay;"
Now that soul is gone to bliss,
With such joy as the angels' is,
  More than I can say.
This child thanked God Almight,
And his mother, Mary bright,
  That he had seen that day;
Then to Bristowe is he gone,
In his shirt and breech alone,
  He had no clothës gay.

When the burgess the child did see,
He said: "Benedicite!
  What array is this, my sone?"
"Truly, master," said the child,
"I am come myself to yield
  To be your bondësman:
Whatsoever ye put me to,
I with all my might shall do,
  While my life shall last."
The burgess marvelled at the sight:
"How camest thou in such a plight?
  Tell me what hath past.

" For the old love twixt thee and me,
Tell me, sone, how it stands with thee,
    Why thou goest in such array?"
"Sir, all my goods I have sold, iwiss,
To get my father to heavenly bliss,
    For sooth as I you say;
For there was no man but me
His attorney that wolde be
    At his dying day."
Then he told his master dear
How oft his father did appear,
    And also in what way.

" And now his soul I have seen to bliss
Convoyëd by the angelës,
    May God thy guerdon send!
For through thy treasure he is safe,
And I his derë blessing have;
    My cares are at an end."
" Sone," he said, " may God thee bless,
That woldst thyself make penniless
    Thy father to redeem:
Speak thine honor may all mankind;
Such trusty friends are hard to find,
    So true as thou to him."

His master said: "I shall thee tell:
Thou knowest how to buy and sell;
   Here now I makë thee
Mine own partner in everywise,
Of worldly goods and merchandise,
   For thy fidelity.
Also I have none in mine age
To receive mine heritage,
   Of my body born to me;
Here I make thee now mine heir,
Of all my landës good and fair;
   Be thou *mine* attorney."

His master had him wedded soon
To a man's daughter of that town
   Who was of worthy race,
And when his master dear was dead,
Into all his goods he enterëd,
   Chattels, lands, and place.
Thus hath this young man outlived his care,
First was rich, and after bare,
   Then richer than ever he was:
Now he that made both hell and heaven,
And all the world, in dayës seven,
   Grant us all his grace!